COPYCAT DOG

Written by Michael J. Pellowski
Illustrated by Anne Kennedy

Troll Asso

Library of Congress Cataloging in Publication Data

Pellowski, Michael.
    Copycat dog.

    Summary: Monty, a Saint Bernard dog from the city,
tries to adjust to life on a farm by imitating the
other animals there.
    [1. Saint Bernard dog—Fiction. 2. Dogs—Fiction.
3. Farm life—Fiction. 4. Domestic animals—Fiction]
I. Kennedy, Anne, 1955-   ill. II. Title.
PZ7.P3656Co   1986   [E]   85-14128
ISBN 0-8167-0652-2 (lib. bdg.)
ISBN 0-8167-0653-0 (pbk.)

10   9   8   7   6   5   4   3   2   1

COPYCAT
DOG

A big city is a very special place. It is a nice place to live. Mr. Floyd lived in the city. He liked living in the big city.

Mr. Floyd had a car. It was a special little car. A little car is good to have in a big city.

What else did Mr. Floyd have?
He had a dog. The dog was
special, too. His name was
Monty.

Why was Monty special? Monty was big. He was very, very big.

Monty was a very nice dog. He was a good dog. But he was too big!

He was too big for Mr. Floyd's
little car. Monty was too big for
lots of things in the city. A big
city is not a good place for a big
dog.

"Monty needs a special place,"
said Mr. Floyd. "A farm is a
good place for a big, big dog.
My friend, Mr. McGee, is a
farmer. He needs a dog. I will
give him my dog."

Mr. Floyd called Monty.
"Monty, you are not a city dog,"
he said. "I will give you to
Farmer McGee. He is good and
kind. You will like being a farm
dog."

Monty liked Mr. Floyd. But he did not like the big city. He thought he would like to live on a farm. Mr. Floyd got in his little car. Monty squeezed in, too. Away they went to Mr. McGee's farm.

The farm was a nice place. It
had a nice farmhouse. It had a
big barn. It had lots of farm
animals.

Farmer McGee was very
friendly.
"I like big dogs," he said. "A big
dog is just what I need."
Monty liked Farmer McGee.

Mr. Floyd got back in his
little car.
"Goodbye, Monty," said Mr.
Floyd. "Goodbye, Farmer
McGee."
Back to the big city went Mr.
Floyd.

Farmer McGee looked at Monty.
"I must go to work," he said.
"See you at supper time. Be a
good farm dog."
Away he went to do his work.

Poor Monty! How could he be a
good farm dog? He did not
know about farms. He did not
know about farm animals.
Monty did not know what to do!

Monty went into the big barn.
"*Who?* Who is that?" called a
little owl.
Monty looked up at the owl.
"I am Monty," said the dog.
"Are you a farm animal?"

"I am a barn owl," said the owl.
"What kind of animal are you?"
Monty looked down.
"I am a city dog. But I want to
be a farm dog. How can I be
like the other farm animals?"

"Monty see, Monty do," called
the owl.
"What?" said Monty.
The owl called, "Monty see,
Monty do. Look at the farm
animals. See what they do.
Then Monty see, Monty do."

"Monty see, Monty do," said the
dog. "That is the way to be a
farm dog. Goodbye, little owl."
Monty left the barn.

A farm animal was by the barn.
It was a chicken. The chicken
was scratching in the dirt.
Scratch! Scratch! Scratch!
Chickens like to scratch in the
dirt. Chickens scratch for their
supper.

Monty looked at the chicken
scratching. Monty see, Monty
do. Monty scratched like a
chicken, too. What a silly thing
for a big dog to do!

The chicken stopped scratching.
Monty stopped, too. The
chicken went to a nest. In the
nest were eggs. The chicken sat
on the nest.

What about Monty? Monty see,
Monty do. He went up to a nest
of eggs. Monty sat down.
Goodbye, eggs!
Crack! Crack! Crack!

Poor, poor Monty! Sitting on cracked eggs is not very comfortable. Monty got up. Away he went.

"I do not like scratching," said Monty. "And I do not like sitting on a nest. But I want to be a good farm dog."

Monty looked for other farm
animals. He saw some goats.
The goats were butting their
heads together. Goats like to
butt. They have special hard
heads for butting.

How about Monty? Monty see,
Monty do. Monty went to butt
heads with a big goat.

CRACK! Into the dirt went
Monty. Poor, poor Monty!

Monty scratched his head.
"Butting is not good for a dog,"
he said.
And away he went.

Monty went to the fields behind
the farmhouse. Rows and rows
of corn were growing there.

In the corn stood a scarecrow.
Big black crows like to eat corn.
A scarecrow's job is to scare the
crows away. But Monty did not
know about scarecrows.

"Is that a farm animal?" said
Monty.
Monty stood and looked.
The big dog said, "Monty see,
Monty do."
Monty did.

Out in the corn stood Monty.
He stood like a scarecrow. But a
big dog is not a good scarecrow.
Monty did not scare crows away
from the corn.

Big black crows scratched for
corn. They ate the corn. Crows
were everywhere. They were
even on Monty's head. Crows!
Crows! Crows! Poor, poor
Monty!

Farmer McGee's cows went by
the corn. The cows scared the
crows. Away went the crows.
But Monty stood and stood.

The cows were going back to
the barn. It was time for their
supper.

Monty looked at the cows. He looked and stood and stood and looked.

The cows went by. Monty see,
Monty do. Monty went after the
cows. The cows went to the
barn. Monty went, too.

At the barn was Farmer McGee.
He saw the cows. Behind the
cows, he saw Monty.

"Monty is bringing the cows to the barn," said Farmer McGee. "What good work! What a good farm dog."

The cows went in the barn.
They ate corn for their supper.

Up came Monty. Farmer McGee
looked at the big dog.
"Good dog, Monty," said
Farmer McGee. "I need a dog to
bring the cows to the barn. You
are just the dog I need."

Now Monty knew what to do.
He knew how to be a good farm
dog.

"It is time for supper," said
Farmer McGee.
He went to the farmhouse.
Monty went, too.

"Here is my supper," said
Farmer McGee. "Here is your
supper, Monty."

Supper looked very good to
Monty. Being a farm dog was
hard work. And big dogs like to
eat. They like to eat a lot.

Monty looked at Farmer McGee.
He was eating supper. And what
about Monty?
Monty see, Monty do!